Hi! I'm Betty. I'm a baby because I am just five days old.
It is nice to meet you!

Many bumble bees live underground, but I was born inside this round bee building that sits beside the shed. A nice man named Builder Bryce made it for our colony.

Bouncing
Baby Bumble Bee

For fun see if you can find this ladybug
on each page of the story

By Doc Goodhe♥rt
Illustrated by Anastasiia Saikova

Doc and Ellie Goodheart are authors of children's
books. They are located in the USA, and are
blessed to bring reading joy to you and yours.

Bouncing Baby Bumble Bee is an original story by Doc Goodheart
based on his love of nature growing up. With this book the goal is to
show how important it is for those around us to be encouraging,
and for us to try things even when they seem hard.

Doc and Ellie wish
to put smiles on faces and make many good
hearts happy.

Published by Hear Me Read, LLC.
HearMeReadLLC@gmail.com
ISBN: 978-1-953604-16-3
Copyright © 2021 by Doc Goodheart

A colony is like a small town for bumble bees.
We have a special leader, our queen bumble bee.
We bring her food so she will lay eggs and have babies.

I'm a type of bumble bee called Broken-belted. Can you see where my big yellow belt doesn't quite make it all the way around?

Today is my day to learn how to fly! I am so excited.
Will you be excited with me?

It is the job of every bumble bee to collect pollen from flowers. See the bumble bees kissing each flower? Mom says it's not our job, but our joy to love on the flowers.

Other things can also fly. Can you find them in this picture?

Now about flying. My daddy, they call him Big Boy Bubba, says to flap my wings really fast. Even a bee his size can fly.

My mom, Beautiful Bella, says I will just figure it out.
It is something called "insect instinct".

Some plants can only make fruit by the special 'buzz' pollen collecting bumble bees can do. Not even our cousins the honey bees can do it. One of these fruits is blueberries.

I'm nervous about flying. What if it is too hard? What if I fall and it hurts? My mom says it is the job of the girls and women to collect pollen. She has faith that I will fly.

I'm standing on the ground and ready to try to fly for the first time. Can you shout, "Fly Betty fly?"

My wings are flapping and my heart is pounding.
Buzz, buzz go my wings. Will I fly?

I am lifting off the ground, just a little. I lean forward, so I go straight ahead. And then things start to get strange.

I go to the left and then to the right. I am out of control.
I do a somersault and crash into the ground.

Everyone watching shouts 'Crash landing!' and cheers. I thought I failed, yet everyone is excited and cheering for me.

Go Betty go! Fly Betty fly! Almost there Betty. You will do it next time, or the next. You are so good at this. With all the excitement I jump into the air and flap my wings.

Up, up I go. Oh no! I am coming back down. I bounce off the ground and back into the air! Down then up. Up then down. I bounce and fly, fly and bounce. I'm doing it! I'm bounce-flying!

The crowd is cheering loud now. Builder Bryce, Big Boy Bubba, Beautiful Bella all cheering for the bouncing baby broken-belt bumble bee! Will you cheer for me too?

Boing, bounce, boing, bounce I go. And now I'm kissing a flower.

With practice I am now able to fly. Kissing and loving the flowers. Fantastic. Thank you for your help and cheering for me too!

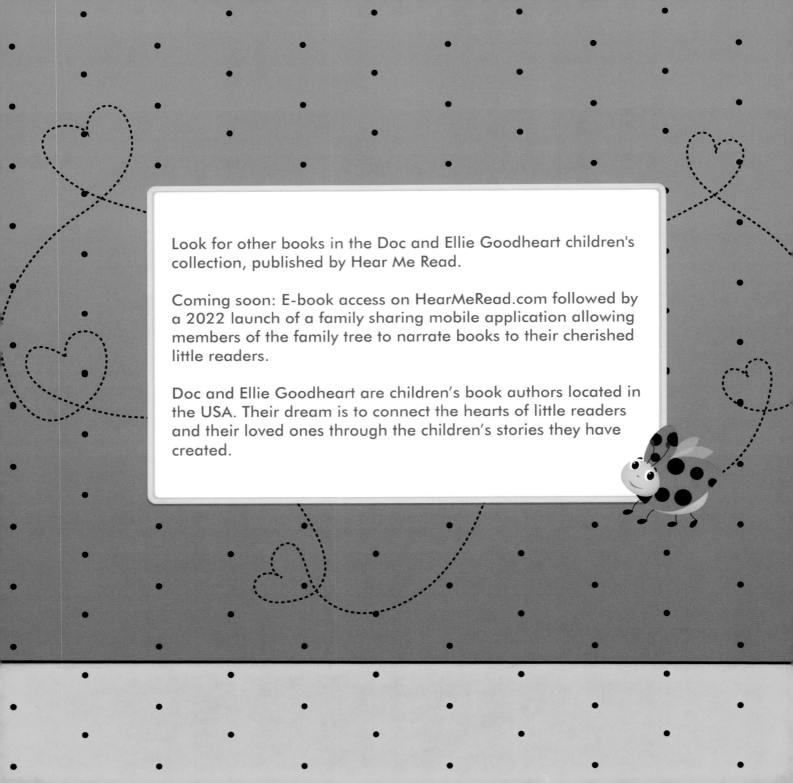

Look for other books in the Doc and Ellie Goodheart children's collection, published by Hear Me Read.

Coming soon: E-book access on HearMeRead.com followed by a 2022 launch of a family sharing mobile application allowing members of the family tree to narrate books to their cherished little readers.

Doc and Ellie Goodheart are children's book authors located in the USA. Their dream is to connect the hearts of little readers and their loved ones through the children's stories they have created.

Made in the USA
Middletown, DE
16 February 2022